Let's Go
SNOWBOARDING

Suzanne Slade

PowerKiDS
press™

New York

To Patrick, who enjoys bustin' carves in the early morning corduroy with his chopper

Published in 2007 by The Rosen Publishing Group, Inc.
29 East 21st Street, New York, NY 10010

First Edition

Editor: Amelie von Zumbusch
Book Design: Dean Galiano and Erica Clendening
Layout Design: Julio Gil

Photo Credits: Cover, p. 7 © www.istockphoto.com/Christian Sawicki; pp. 4, 12 © www.istockphoto.com/Maxim Pertrichuk; pp. 5, 6, 16, 18 © www.shutterstock.com; pp. 8, 22, 23, 24, 25, 26, 28 © Getty Images; p. 10 © www.istockphoto.com/Michael Chen; p. 11 © www.istockphoto.com/Mira Janacek; p. 15 © www.istockphoto.com/Ben Renard-Wiart; p. 20 © www.istockphoto.com/Tobias Tuleby; p. 21 © www.istockphoto.com/Jacom Stephens.

Library of Congress Cataloging-in-Publication Data

Slade, Suzanne.
  Let's go snowboarding / Suzanne Slade. — 1st ed.
     p. cm. — (Adventures outdoors)
  Includes index.
  ISBN-13: 978-1-4042-3648-6 (library binding)
  ISBN-10: 1-4042-3648-1 (library binding)
  1. Snowboarding—Juvenile literature. I. Title.
  GV857.S57S53 2007
  796.93'9—dc22
                                        2006019563

Manufactured in the United States of America

Contents

The Sport of Snowboarding

Which sport is like skateboarding without wheels, surfing without water, or skiing without two skis? The answer is snowboarding. Snowboarding has certain things in common with other sports, but nothing else is quite like it. Nothing can compare to the excitement and huge rush that snowboarders experience.

Snowboarding is one of the fastest-growing sports in the world. People enjoy the freedom of racing over

Snowboarders can speed down the mountainside.

beautiful white **powder** and the fun of learning new tricks. Snowboarders have a style all their own. They glide down snow-covered mountains with grace. They carve, or turn, with ease. They show their individuality and bravery with speed and high air tricks. Anyone can learn to snowboard and enjoy the thrills of this exciting sport.

Snowboarders do many different tricks high in the air.

Snowboarding Gear

It's important to use the proper gear when you go snowboarding. There are three types of snowboards. They are alpine boards, freestyle boards, and freeride boards. A board that looks cool is great, but you need to choose the right type of board for you.

Alpine boards are stiff and narrow. Racers like this board because it is fast and makes high-speed turns.

Many snowboarders wear goggles to keep wind, snow, and the sun's glare out of their eyes.

A freestyle board is wider and is used for jumping and special tricks. Most beginners use a freeride board. It handles well and can also be used for doing tricks. Snowboard bindings hold your feet in place. You should wear snowboard boots when boarding. Always wear a helmet, thick snowboarding gloves, and a leash that connects your board to your boot.

Snowboard bindings are fastened directly to a snowboarder's boots.

Where to Snowboard

The best place to go snowboarding is a ski **resort**. Resorts have **rope tows** and **chair lifts** to carry you up hills. They also have several different levels of **runs**.

Each downhill run has a label to indicate how challenging it is. A green circle means a short, gentle trail that was made for beginners. These trails are a great place to start snowboarding. A run with a blue square is longer, steeper, and more challenging. A black diamond run is a steep trail for advanced boarders and skiers. Some black diamonds have moguls, which are small bumps on the hill.

Most resorts have a special area called a **terrain** park for practicing snowboard tricks. Terrain parks have **rails** and jumps for doing air tricks.

These snowboarders are riding the ski lift at Park City Mountain Resort, in Park City, Utah.

Getting on the Board

Snowboarding may not feel natural at first. New boarders often feel unsteady while sliding down a hill with both feet fastened to a board. To avoid spending more time sitting on the snow than gliding over it, you could take a lesson.

An instructor will show you how to stand sideways on the board. Make sure to keep your front hand

It is a good idea to practice standing on a snowboard before you head down the slopes.

over the **nose** and your other hand behind for balance. You'll learn how to dig the edge of your board into the snow to turn, slow down, or stop. It's also important to know how to fall without landing on your hands.

When falling backward, you should land on your backside. If you fall forward, tuck in your elbows and land on your arms.

Learning how to fall safely is an important part of learning how to snowboard.

Freeriding

Freeriding is snowboarding just for fun. You can freeride through all types of mountain terrain, such as soft powder or packed snow. Freeriders don't worry about doing tricks or going fast, they just cut loose and go boarding.

You can sideslip to slow down while you are freeriding. To sideslip your board must be at a right angle to the downhill slope of the hill as you dig the edge of the board that is farthest uphill into the snow. A heelside sideslip is when you are looking down a hill and you dig your heel edge into the snow. If you are facing uphill, you can toe sideslip by pushing the edge of the board that is under your toes into the snow.

This snowboarder is doing a heelside sideslip.

Backcountry Boarding

Backcountry boarding is when you ride your board in areas outside a ski resort. The first snowboarders had to backcountry board because snowboards were not allowed at resorts.

Backcountry boarders often use a split-board. This type of snowboard breaks apart into two pieces. You can walk up the mountain with one piece fastened to each shoe. At the top the pieces are snapped together to make a snowboard. After a long hike, a snowboarder is rewarded with untouched snow. Some boarders hire a **helicopter** or **snowcat** to take them up to the top of backcountry trails.

This backcountry snowboarder has just jumped off a snowy cliff.

Alpine Snowboarding

Alpine boarding is a high-speed sport. In this type of snowboarding, the rider makes fast carved turns. These carved turns make cuts in the snow and leave a curved trail on the hill.

A stiff alpine board bends slightly when a boarder makes a turn. One side of the snowboard touches the snow and cuts, or carves, a turn. An alpine board is curved on each side, making it narrow in the middle. These curved areas are called sidecuts. Alpine boarders wear hard plastic boots for extra control. They also usually point their feet more toward the front of the board than other types of snowboarders.

Alpine snowboarding is sometimes known as hardboot snowboarding.

Freestyle

Freestyle snowboarding is all about putting on a great show. Freestyle boarders do tricks on the snow and up high in the air. They use their snowboarding skills, timing, and personal style to create a performance that people love to watch.

Many freestyle tricks have come from skateboarding. The ollie is a basic skateboard and freestyle move. The move has a series of motions that must be carefully timed. To perform an ollie, put your weight on the snowboard's tail, or back end, while you lift up the front of the board and then jump.

DID YOU KNOW?

Snowboarders make up names for different tricks. Many tricks are named after foods, such as the burger flip, roast beef air, swiss cheese air, McEgg, chicken salad air, and eggflip.

An ollie is the trick snowboarders most often use to get their boards into the air.

This snowboarder is doing a melon grab.

A frontside spin is when you jump in the air and do a turn while looking downhill. If you jump and turn so that you are facing uphill, you are doing a backside spin. A trick called a grab is when you grab your board with one or two hands while you are in the air. There are many different grabs, such as nose grabs, tail grabs, and melon grabs. To do a melon, grab your board's heel edge with your front hand.

Doing a tail wheelie is similar to doing a wheelie on a bike. To do this trick, stand on the tail of the board and push the nose up. Riding fakie means you ride your board in the opposite direction from the way you usually do. For example, if you usually put your left foot forward, turn your body the other way and board with your right foot forward to ride fakie.

To do a tail grab, grab onto the tail of your snowboard with your rear hand.

Snowboarding Competitions

Snowboarders travel all over the world to compete in events such as the halfpipe, slalom, and boardercross. Boarders speed down round walls in the halfpipe. When they get to the top of a wall, they jump high in the air and do tricks. In the slalom riders race around **gates** while boarding downhill. During boardercross, four to six riders race down a challenging course with gates and jumps.

Mellie Francon, Lindsey Jacobellis, and Karine Ruby competed in boardercross at the 2006 Olympics.

The biggest snowboarding competitions, or contests, are the X Games, the World Championship, the U.S. Open, and the Olympics. Snowboarding became an Olympic sport at the 1998 Winter Games in Nagano, Japan. Halfpipe and slalom events for both men and women were included. Men's and women's boardercross events were added at the 2006 Games in Turin, Italy.

American snowboarder Chris Klug raced in slalom events at the 1988 and 2002 Olympics.

Famous Boarders

The best snowboarders in the world spend a lot of time practicing on their boards. Shaun White, from California, is one of the top male snowboarders. He is called the Flying Tomato because of his long, red hair. Shaun won the gold **medal** in men's halfpipe at the 2006 Winter Olympic

Shaun White and Hannah Teter were both 19 when they won gold medals at the 2006 Olympics.

Seth Wescott is the snowboarder in the center of this picture from the 2006 Olympics.

Games. He has earned many medals in X Games competitions. Seth Wescott is among the best boardercross riders. He won gold medals at the 2005 World Championship and the 2006 Olympics.

Hannah Teter was raised in a family of snowboarders in Vermont. She is one of the world's best halfpipe riders. Hannah won gold at the 2006 Olympics, bronze at the 2005 World Championship, and finished first in the 2004 Winter X Games.

Snowboarding and Nature

Along with the excitement of racing over snow and flying through the air, snowboarders enjoy the beauty of nature. While standing at the top of a mountain or riding up a chair lift, boarders are surrounded by some of the most wonderful views in the world. Stately green pines, clear blue skies, and pure white snow are everywhere they look. People who snowboard on backcountry trails may also see interesting wild animals, such as deer, rabbits, eagles, and other types of birds.

Boarders love to be outside. They value the natural scenery they see when they snowboard. Wherever they go to **catch fat air** or **cut up the corduroy**, snowboarders always leave the area just as clean and beautiful as they found it.

This snowboarder is looking out over the mountains in Whistler, British Columbia.

Let's Go Snowboarding!

Snowboarding is a great way to have fun while you get exercise. Every year more and more people are learning to board. Boarders enjoy the warmth of the sun as they carve down a mountain or fly through the air. You'll never get bored on a snowboard. There are always new tricks and jumps you can try. You can use your creativity in this sport and invent your own move.

So grab your best buddy, rent a board, and sign up for a lesson together. With the right gear and a little practice, you can enjoy snowboarding, too. When you head for the hills, you'll surely have a few hard spills and lots of fast thrills.

Let's go snowboarding!

It's always a good idea to go snowboarding with a friend. You never know what might happen!

Safety Tips

- Wear proper safety gear, such as a helmet, padded snowboard pants, wrist guards, and goggles, while snowboarding.

- Fasten your snowboard to your boot or leg with a leash. A loose board can slide quickly down a hill and hit someone.

- Always snowboard with a buddy. Keep track of where your friend is while you are boarding.

- Stay on the marked and maintained trails. There may be big rocks, trees, or deep holes called crevasses in the areas outside of the resort.

- Practice new skills and work up to them slowly. Do not try a trick until you are prepared for it.

- Be sure to drink plenty of water while you are boarding.

- Keep plenty of distance between you and other skiers and snowboarders. Always remember that someone in front of you may change direction suddenly.

- Slow down when you reach the bottom of the hill or as you come near a lift line. Someone can get hurt if you try to stop suddenly near people.

- Obey signs that mark a closed trail or unsafe area.

- Pull off on the side of the trail if you want to take a rest while snowboarding.

Glossary

catch fat air (KACH FAT ER) To do exciting tricks in the air.

chair lifts (CHER LIFTS) Lines of seats that hang from a cable and carry people up a mountain.

cut up the corduroy (KUT UP THUH KOR-duh-roy) To snowboard through the bumpy lines left by machines that ski resorts use to smooth out slopes.

gates (GAYTS) Poles that people race around or between.

helicopter (HEH-luh-kop-ter) An aircraft that is kept in the air by blades that spin above the craft.

medal (MEH-dul) A small, round piece of metal given as a prize.

nose (NOHZ) The front end of a snowboard.

powder (POW-dur) Loose snow.

rails (RAYLZ) Flat, metal bars for snowboards to glide on.

resort (rih-ZORT) A place people go to have fun and relax.

rope tows (ROHP TOHZ) Moving ropes that pull people up a slope.

runs (RUNZ) Trails or slopes that have been prepared for skiing or snowboarding.

snowcat (SNOH-kat) A tracked truck that moves on snow.

terrain (tuh-RAYN) A piece of land or the qualities of a piece of land.

Index

Web Sites

Due to the changing nature of Internet links, PowerKids Press has developed an online list of Web sites related to this book. This site is updated regularly. Please use this link to access the list: www.powerkidslinks.com/adout/snowboard/